Hunting Stefan

Thomas Blackwell

ISBN: 978-1-80645-025-1
Published by Thomas Blackwell Publishing

This story contains themes related to mental health. It is intended for mature readers.

For the minds that rebuild themselves
while something in the dark watches and waits...

Prologue: The Space Between

They told me it was over.

That the man I thought I knew, the man who buried me and called it love, was gone.

They say I am safe now.

But no one tells you what happens after survival.

No one explains that when you claw your way out of the dark, the dark comes with you. It gets under your skin, seeps into your eyes, a slow infection you can't cut out. Sometimes, in the mirror, I still see him. Not his face exactly, just the shape of him, the shadow that fits where mine used to be.

The police asked me for a name. I told them "Neil." Then "Stefan." Then nothing at all, because the truth is I don't know which version of him was real, or which part of me survived.

At night I dream of the meadow, the one I could see calm him. In the dream the stream runs red, and the tree at the edge of the field, black against a sky that never turns to morning. Sometimes I wake up with the taste of dirt in my mouth, as if I've been crawling again.

The Doctors call it post-traumatic stress. I call it remembering.

Because I know he's still out there. Or he's in here, somewhere beneath the skin, whispering through my heartbeat. Either way, I can feel him watching.

I've stopped waiting for the nightmares to fade. I've started following them.

If I can find him, find Stefan, maybe I can finally remember which part of me he killed that night. And finally meet what rose in its place.

Chapter 1
Awakening in Ash

Jane jolted upright, gasping. The phantom sensation of dirt filled her mouth, thick and suffocating. Stefan's cold laughter echoed in her ears, that cruel, familiar sound that had haunted her nightmares since the burial. She could still feel his hands shoving her into the grave, see the moonlight glinting off the shovel as he buried her alive beside Emily's bones.

They told me it was over. That he was gone. But the mind does not heal on command. Sometimes I still wake up tasting soil, like the earth hasn't decided if it has finished with me yet.

Her heart hammered against her ribs like a trapped bird. Sweat plastered her hair to her forehead, cold and clammy in the stale air. Janes eyes adjusting to the dim light as weak moonlight strained through layers of newspaper taped over the windows, casting fractured shadows across the bare walls forcing jane to hold her breathe as she comes to realise they are not a threat. This safehouse felt more like a tomb, a far cry from the sunlit apartment she'd shared with the monster she thought was Neil.

Jane swung her legs over the edge of the narrow bed, her bare feet hitting the cold concrete floor. She pressed her palms flat against her knees to stop the trembling. She couldn't help but feel that Stefan was near, lurking in the shadows, stalking her again, just waiting for his chance to strike. The nightmare had felt too real, the damp earth, the skeletal fingers brushing hers as she clawed through the grave, Stefan's breath hot on her neck.

"You can't hide forever."

Jane could almost smell the scent of his cologne in the air, a cologne he only used for special occasions, a deep musky scent, a scent she adored on him, the one she used to borrow when she wanted to feel close to him, now it makes her stomach churn. Jane shook her head to try and wake herself up and get rid of the scent. She thought to herself, it's funny how survival takes away pleasure and twists it into nausea.

She stumbled toward the bathroom, guided by memory in the near, dark. The door groaned on its hinges. Inside, the single bulb flickered weakly when she yanked the chain. Her reflection in the cracked mirror startled her; hollow eyes, tangled hair, the fading memory of the bruises along her jawline from her escape through the woods. A ghost of Jane stared back at her in the mirror.

Jane traced the dark circles beneath her eyes. Jane wondered when she became so thin, when did her eyes begin to sink into the darkness around them. This wasn't the woman who'd laughed over Thai takeout with Neil....Stefan, she corrected herself, the name bitter as ash. That Jane had been soft curves and hopeful smiles. This creature was sharp angles and haunted eyes. She'd lost more than her apartment, her job, her naive trust. She'd lost the unshakable certainty that the world held safe places. That sunlight through leaves was just sunlight. That love wasn't camouflage for predation.

The weight of it pressed down, heavier than the dirt that had filled her grave. It felt like a story she'd read about someone else. Now, every shadow pulsed with latent threat, every silence screamed with unspoken terror. Her hands shook as she splashed icy water on her face, the cold a feeble anchor back to reality.

Jane gripped the edges of the sink, her knuckles whitening against the chipped porcelain, trying to anchor herself, whether to reality or simply to remain standing, she couldn't tell. The face in the mirror blurred….not just hers, but Emily's hollow stare, the terrified eyes of ghosts Stefan had buried beneath his twisted shrine. Preserved forever as a memory. He hadn't just stolen her future; he'd poisoned her past, turning every cherished moment with *Neil* into a calculated lie.

The warmth of his embrace? A trap.

The whispered promises? Blueprints for her coffin.

The gentleness of his touch? Hands that dug her grave

The rage ignited, sudden and volcanic, burning through the icy dread. It was not fear tightening her chest anymore; it was pure, incandescent fury. This was not living. This was hiding. Existing in newspaper, filtered twilight, jumping at every creak, haunted by a ghost who was not dead.

He did this. The thought screamed inside her skull. *He made me this trembling shadow*.

Her reflection seemed to sneer back, weak, broken, his creation. The pressure built, unbearable, a scream trapped behind clenched teeth. One fist clenched tighter. Then, without thought, only raw, shattering fury, she drove it forward.

The mirror shattered, the ghosts of her past disappeared, a jagged spiderweb exploding across the glass. Shards rained into the sink, glittering like frozen tears in the gloom. Pain bloomed hot and sharp across her knuckles, blood welling crimson against the pale porcelain. She gasped, the shock of impact anchoring her back to the damp, silent bathroom. To the sticky warmth on her skin. To the jagged pieces reflecting a fractured Jane back at her.

Each shard of mirror held a sliver of her face, eyes wide, lips parted, not in terror this time, but in stunned, breathless defiance. The silence roared louder than the breaking glass. Slowly, deliberately, she turned her bleeding hand over, watching the blood bead and drip. The sting was real. The anger was real. She was real. Not preserved. Not a memory. Not his. Stefan had not buried her. Not really. Not yet.

And rage, she realized with a clarity sharp as the glass, was a far better fuel than fear. It burned hotter. It didn't freeze you in the dark. It forged you.

She stared at the wreckage below, breathing hard. The trembling hadn't stopped, but its source had shifted. This wasn't the tremble of prey. This was the tremor of something waking up. Something dangerous. Something unburied.

As her gaze lifted from the bleeding knuckles and the shattered glass beneath, she stared upon the mirror in front, and among the fractured reflections, one piece caught her eye clearly. It showed her eyes, not haunted, not broken but blazing. Alive. Purposefully alive.

She leant closer, ignoring the sting. The face staring back was not Jane the victim anymore. It was something fiercer. Something Stefan had not buried deep enough.

A grim, determined smile touched her lips. He had won that night. He had killed the soft, hopeful woman who believed in coffee shop miracles and safe embraces. That Jane lay rotting under Emily's tree.

But if jane was dead, then what crawled out? A hollow being choked by terror, flinching at shadows, jumping at creaks. A walking tomb. Until now. Until this rage.

It was not just anger; it was wildfire. It scorched the fear, burned away the trembling uncertainty. It filled the hollow places Stefan had carved out, not with hope, but with molten resolve. He had not just taken her trust; he had taken the tools of a blacksmith and hammered her carefully and precisely and forged her into the shape he desired.

Fine, Jane felt resolve settle over her. Stefan had been the master of this creation; let him reap what he sowed. This new creature in the mirror? It did not flinch. It hunted.

Chapter 2
Rebirth in Blood

Blood traced delicate paths down the glass, thin red threads glinting under the flickering bulb. It looked almost deliberate, a portrait painted in pain and reflection.

Jane stared, unblinking. Her breath came in small, uneven bursts, fogging the fractured surface until her face disappeared, then returned again...broken into a hundred pieces. Her chest ached from the effort of breathing. Her heartbeat thundered too loudly in her skull, drowning out the world beyond these walls. And then something inside her, something fragile and exhausted, simply gave way. A soft, invisible snap.

Her gaze shifted downward. On the cluttered sink, amid the shards of glass and streaks of red, lay a small pair of scissors, rusted at the hinge, dull from years of use. Her fingers found them without thought, guided by something primal.

The first cut was clumsy. Her hair tugged against the blunt blade, resisting before surrendering with a sound like tearing silk. A thick lock tumbled into the sink, sticking to her blood smeared hand. She watched it fall, detached, almost curious. Another cut followed, then another. The snipping became rhythmic, mechanical, hypnotic. Hair slid down her arms, across her bare shoulders, gathering in dark clumps at her feet. With every strand that fell, something lighter rose in her chest, something wild and trembling, like laughter trying to claw its way out.

When she paused, breathless, her reflection was already changing. The woman who looked back was someone new, someone wilder. Hair uneven, jagged. Eyes sunken, fever bright. Lips pale and trembling. Jane, the woman the world had known, was already a ghost, was already dead.

She tilted her head. The scissors glinted in the weak light. She pressed the edge to her cheek, just below the bone. The blade trembled with her hand. A single breath in, out and then she dragged it gently downward. A shallow cut bloomed crimson. It did not hurt the way she thought it would. The pain was clean. Real. Controlled.

She let the blood bead, slide down her jaw, the blood gathers in the sink below, dark and shining. Each drop lands with a soft, hollow tap against the porcelain. Another cut, deeper. A mirror of the first. A mark of ownership. Her beauty, that naive, delicate thing that had once charmed the monster was gone. She had carved it out herself. The pain a stark reminder she is still alive. Her reflection almost screaming at her to stop but she could not allow herself to be that weak. The blood gathers in the sink below, dark and shining. A baptism of her own making. Blood christens the wound, the cut will heal but the scar will remain. It will belong to her.

The girl the monster loved is gone.

Something harder is being born in her place and this time it will belong only to her.

The mirror flickered as the bulb overhead stuttered again, and for an instant, she thought she saw him in the reflection. Stefan. Smiling. Watching. Her stomach twisted.

“Not anymore,” she whispered to the glass. “You don’t get to look at me anymore.”

The bulb hummed, steadied. His image vanished, leaving only her blood smeared reflection.

Jane stripped her clothes, the fabric sticking to her sweat damp skin, and stepped beneath the shower. The pipes coughed and spat before surrendering to a harsh stream. The water ran brown at first, rust, dust, old ghosts, before turning scalding. She stood in it, head bowed, letting it burn. The water hit her cuts and ignited them with pain. She did not move. The sting was purifying. Steam rose, blurring the cracked mirror, wrapping her in a shroud of mist.

She imagined it washing away the dirt from the grave, the sweat of fear, the fingerprints he had left on her skin. She could almost hear his voice, low and coaxing “You can’t hide forever.” Her fingers clenched into fists.

“I’m not hiding,” she hissed through her teeth.

The water spiralled red at her feet. Blood, hair, and sweat twisting together before disappearing down the drain, carrying past Jane with it. The hiss of the shower became the sound of rain, and with it came memories. The hospital. The white lights. The smell of antiseptic and decay. She remembered the detective, grey suit, kind eyes that never quite met hers, sitting at the edge of her bed.

“We recovered remains,” he said gently. “Forensics has confirmed the identity as Emily.”

She had felt nothing. Not relief. Not grief. Just a hollow echo where emotion should have been.

The detective had told her they’d gone to the address she’d given. The apartment. The place where Stefan had smiled at her across candlelight, brushed hair from her cheek, kissed her forehead and promised her forever. But when the police arrived, there was nothing. Empty walls. No furniture. No life. No blood. No trace he had ever existed.

The detectives spoke in clinical tones. "We have searched every record. No legal name matches Stefan Brown. No Neil Hartman in the system. It is like he never existed."

But Jane knew better. He had not vanished. He had shed his skin.

And the police… she felt their doubt like a weight pressing against her. They suspected her. That Stefan was a figment, a story she had conjured. That she might have killed Emily herself. They had questioned her, carefully, indirectly, trying to find cracks, searching for a way to pin the truth, or the lie, on her. But of course, they could not tie her to Emily's death. Yet the suspicion lingered, unspoken, like a shadow behind their eyes. They never honestly believed her.

She had begged them to keep looking. To believe her. They had nodded with practiced empathy, then buried her case under red tape and empty condolences. And so, they laid her to rest with the rest of it.

Jane Avery, victim. Deceased. Forgotten. Fine. Let the world forget her.

She gathered the photos and slipped them into a worn folder, tucking it under her arm. The movement was slow, deliberate, ritualistic. Every gesture now felt like a vow. When she spoke, her voice barely rose above a whisper.

"No more graves."

Outside, thunder rumbled far off, rolling across the horizon like a promise.

Jane blew out the last candle on the table. The room plunged into shadow, broken only by the faint grey wash of morning. Her heart was steady now. Her purpose absolute. The old Jane had been buried. The hopeful, trusting woman who had believed in the goodness of strangers was gone.

What remained was a creature of instinct and resolve, a revenant forged from earth, blood, and rage.

When she stepped outside, the air was damp and cold, the scent of rain thick in her lungs. She lifted her face to it, letting the droplets streak her skin, washing away any last traces of blood. Each drop felt like a heartbeat. A drumbeat. A summons.

She closed her eyes, breathed deeply, and smiled, a small, crooked thing that didn't reach her eyes.

The hunt had begun…

Chapter 3
Hunted no more

Three months.

Three months circling the Bowery like a ghost haunting its own grave.

Jane knew the odds were stacked against her. Stefan could be in Prague or Buenos Aires by now, sipping espresso and laughing at her futile hunt. But arrogance was his oxygen. Obsession his compass. He would never abandon the stages where he'd orchestrated her terror, Emily's terror. Not completely.

So, she haunted them. The damp brick alleys behind the jazz clubs he had loved. The 24,hour diners where he had spent late evenings. The Restaurants they had spent date nights talking and laughing and enjoying each other's company.

He watched me once. Followed me through every quiet street until I forgot how to move without his eyes. Now I will do the same to him. Maybe this is what surviving really looks like, learning our predators' habits till they become your own.

Her boots wore grooves into the same cracked sidewalks, her eyes scanning faces in the sodium vapor glow.

"Seen him? Tall. Sharp cheekbones. Walks like he owns the pavement."

She slid a grainy photo across the sticky counter of the Deli. The night manager squinted, pushing it back with greasy fingers.

"Lady, this is New York. We got tall guys with cheekbones comin' outta our ears."

Disappointment settled like a stone in her gut, heavy but familiar. She pocketed the sketch carefully, like it was the only proof the man existed beyond her imagination. Every 'no' was a step closer to the yes that would crack this city open. She had learnt that patience wasn't passive, it was a blade being sharpened. And lately, the edge felt dangerously honed.

Her safe house, on the outskirts of the city had become a war room. Maps and photos swallowed the walls, red string webbed across them in obsessive geometry. The Koreatown karaoke bar where he had taken her. The pier where they had walked and laughed, her head tilted back, his arm warm across her shoulders. If she had known then what she knew now, she would have run, run until her lungs split open. But she had not run. She had fallen, deep and stupid, into the gravity of his charm.

Now she traced his routes with the same reverence he once stroked her skin.

Every night, she circled the Bowery, her worn running shoes whispering against rain slick pavement. The hooded cloak swallowed her frame, turning her into a shadow among shadows, her dyed black hair stark against skin gone ashen from sleepless nights and cold fury. Every flicker of movement, a tall man stepping off the curb, a laugh caught in a darkened window, sent her pulse racing. Hope was a jagged thing, cutting her from the inside each time it was not him.

Sometimes, she would park herself across the street from the sleek glass building where she used to work. Through the rain-streaked window of a cheap coffee shop, she would watch them, her old colleagues spilling out after work, laughing, clutching takeout containers, planning rooftop drinks. Life pulsed around them, vibrant and oblivious.

Sarah, her old desk mate, threw her head back in laughter, and Jane felt something cold crawl through her chest. It was not jealousy anymore. It was hunger. For what had been taken. For what she had let be taken. Stefan had not just stolen her life; he'd rewritten it in his own image. And she was learning that revenge was not about justice, it was about authorship. About taking the pen back, one body at a time if she had to.

Tonight, the Bowery felt heavier, the air thick with fried food and exhaust, the neon lights smeared by mist. She leaned against a graffiti tagged dumpster behind one of Stefan's old haunts, the bass from inside vibrating through her ribs.

A group stumbled out the service entrance, laughing, drunk. Jane froze.

Tall. Sharp cheekbones catching the sickly yellow light.

Her breath stopped. Is it him?

The man turned, laughing again, revealing a face too young, eyes too empty. The cold disappointment hit hard, sharper than fear, deeper than grief. She exhaled shakily, tasting metal. The edge of her patience was dulling with every false alarm.

Pushing off the dumpster, she melted back into the alley's throat.

The hunt was a grinding wheel, wearing her down, but also polishing something underneath. Something cleaner. Sharper. She caught her reflection in a rain puddle, hooded, pale, eyes dark and unreadable. For a moment, she did not recognize the woman staring back. There was a calmness there that frightened her, a stillness she remembered from him.

She adjusted her hood, the rough fabric scratching the faint scars along her cheek. They had healed to thin silver lines, reminders of the night she'd marked herself rather than scream. Freedom was not something reclaimed passively; it was seized. And maybe, she thought, freedom had always been a kind of violence.

The city around her pulsed, steam rising from grates, sirens bleeding through fog. Jane moved with the precision of a predator tracing familiar terrain. She knew which streetlights flickered, which alleys dead ended, which corners gave her the best vantage. She had mapped the city the way Stefan once mapped her fear, inch by inch, breath by breath.

She paused under a broken sign, rain whispering down her hood. The air smelled like wet metal and old cigarettes. She could almost hear his voice, low, teasing. *You, see? You are learning.*

And she was.

Three months had carved the Bowery into her bones.

She was not just looking anymore.

She was listening to the heartbeat of the city, to its secrets, to its waiting.

Because one day soon, the city would cough him up. And when it did, Jane would be ready.

Not as his victim. Not as his ghost. But as the thing he made her.

Chapter 4
Echoes in the Dark

The city had its own pulse.

Jane could hear it now.

At first, it was background noise, sirens, rain, the subway's rumble underfoot. But lately, it had rhythm. Breathing. A heartbeat that matched her own.

She had stopped counting days. The calendar was just a blur of marks and crossed out hours. Time felt elastic, stretched thin and translucent. Night melted into morning, then back into night again, until the sky itself seemed confused about what it was supposed to be.

The Bowery was not streets anymore. It was a maze built to test her endurance, walls slick with rain, air thick with the stink of rot and fried grease. Her shoes never fully dried. Her clothes carried the city's scent, a mix of rust, exhaust, and something sourer. She did not mind. It made her harder to track.

She moved differently now, quieter, calculated. She caught herself stepping where the light did not reach, tracing the edges of shadows. She had memorized the intervals of the security cameras along Delancey, the flicker cycle of the neon sign outside the late-night pawn shop, the time it took the bodega owner to dump his trash. It was not stalking anymore. It was choreography.

Sometimes, she thought she could feel Stefan watching her the way she used to feel him in her dreams, not like a ghost, but like gravity. A presence that bent everything toward it.

She had started talking again. Not to people, she couldn't risk that, but to him. Or to herself. The line was getting thin.

"Where are you hiding?" she would whisper into the rain. "You liked this part of the city best, didn't you? Where no one looks twice at a man who smiles too long."

The city never answered. It did not need to. It was already speaking.

Her apartment had shrunk. The walls pressed in with every breath. Maps layered over each other, streets upon streets, a palimpsest of obsession. Pins and thread tangled into red veins that seemed to pulse when the streetlights flickered. Her notes had gone from lists to scribbles, symbols even she struggled to read later.

The table was a graveyard of coffee cups and burned-out candles. A folder of missing persons reports sat in the corner, pages warped by spilled water or maybe sweat. She could not remember.

She had cut her hair again two nights ago. Or maybe three. The scissors had felt heavy, deliberate. The strands clung to her palms like something alive. When she had looked in the mirror afterward, the face staring back was sharper. The eyes looked older, the jaw tighter. There was no fear left there. Just precision.

That evening, she followed a man for almost an hour. He had Stefan's gait, that slow, predatory looseness that seemed careless until you realized it wasn't. She trailed him through two subway changes, across a rain slicked avenue, and into a narrow alley.

He turned. Not Stefan. Just a stranger with tired eyes and an empty cigarette pack. He looked at her like she was dangerous. He was not wrong.

Jane did not apologize. She did not even speak. She just watched him walk away until the sound of his footsteps dissolved into the city's pulse again.

She leaned against the cold brick wall, heart hammering. For a moment, she thought she saw movement at the edge of her vision , a silhouette disappearing into fog. Tall. Familiar. She blinked, and it was gone.

"Where are you Neil….Stefan." correcting herself. "Whatever name you are wearing now, it still lives under my skin".

The rain came harder. The drops hit her face like pinpricks. She tilted her head back and let them. The cold cleared her mind, if only for a breath.

At night, the boundaries softened. Sleep was unreliable, dreams too vivid. In one, she stood in a room lined with mirrors, every reflection a slightly different version of herself, one weeping, one smiling, one holding a knife. She woke up sweating, a metallic taste in her mouth.

When she next woke up, the sun creeping in, she found she'd drawn something in her sleep. A map of the Bowery, sketched in black ink. Her handwriting along the edges read, "He is inside the circle now".

She did not remember writing it. But she believed it.

The city's nights grew meaner, and so did she. Her patience, once sharp, had turned to hunger. She prowled the alleys like a stray dog, scanning faces, reading postures, studying how people moved.

One night, she watched a man rough up a woman outside a club. In the past she may of shouted for help or called someone but she just watched, silent, cold, until he saw her staring and froze. He let go of the woman's arm without a word.

The woman stumbled off into the rain. Jane stayed. The man did not meet her eyes again.

Something about that felt like balance.

She had stopped using her real name. The deli owner called her "Miss Black." The night clerk at the bodega called her "Shadow." It fit. She did not correct them.

Her old life, the job, the laughter, the human version of herself, had drifted too far away to call back. She could barely imagine the sound of her own voice in daylight. When she tried, it sounded wrong. Too soft. Too alive. She did not miss it. Not really. There was power in silence, in precision, in letting go of what slowed you down.

Sometimes, she thought Stefan would be proud of her. That thought should have sickened her. It did not. One night, as she crossed under the Manhattan Bridge, she caught her reflection in a shop window. The hood shadowed her face, hollowing her eyes, tightening her mouth. Stefan's patience, his cold precision, seemed to echo in her posture. He stared back from the glass.

Her breath caught. Then she blinked. Just her again.

But she could not shake the feeling that maybe he wasn't out there anymore. Maybe he was here, wearing her face. The thought did not scare her. It steadied her.

Hours later, she sat in the dark of her apartment, knees drawn up, eyes tracing the glowing web of red thread across the map. Her pulse had slowed. She wasn't chasing him anymore. Not exactly.

She was following something older, something inevitable. And if the path ahead led her somewhere she didn't come back from, so be it.

The city did not need ghosts. It needed hunters.
And Jane, at last, had become one.

Chapter 5
The Mirror's Edge

The rain was falling sideways, driven by wind that howled through the gaps between buildings. The Bowery's pulse was erratic tonight, like a wounded thing trying to steady itself. Jane walked without direction, head down, hood up, the city's reflection running in sheets along the pavement. Every light shimmered. Every sound carried too far.

Then she stopped.

Across the street, a figure cut through the fog. Tall. Broad shouldered. That stride, loose, almost lazy, like someone who never questioned his right to the ground he walked on.

For a moment, she thought her mind was playing another of its tricks. But then he turned, just slightly, and she saw it: the same angular jaw, the same rhythm in the way he scanned his surroundings.

He had changed. His hair was shorter, cropped close to his skull. Darker, almost black now. His skin was darker too, as if sun stained or tinted by disguise. A beard ghosted his jaw, new, unfamiliar. He wore a long coat, different from the ones she remembered, but his movements, those hadn't changed. The subtle control. The precision masked as ease.

And then he turned fully, under the washed-out halo of a streetlight, and she saw his eyes.

That was all it took.

The world tilted, every sound collapsing into the rush of her own heartbeat. For months she had been chasing a ghost, half dreaming his face on strangers in the dark. But this was no mirage. It was him. The way he had looked at her once, love, curiosity, hunger, all those lies braided together in a single glance.

Only now she could see it clearly for what it was.

Not love. Never love.

It was power.

It was ownership.

He had not seen her. Not yet. But she saw him, and that was enough.

He was not alone.

A woman clung to his arm, her laughter thin against the hum of rain and traffic. Young. Brown coat. Pale face haloed by wet hair. The kind of beauty that looked like softness until you realized it was bait.

Jane froze in the doorway of a shuttered shop, heart hammering so hard it blurred her vision. The woman's face caught the light, and something inside Jane twisted. She looked like Emily.

She looked like Jane had, before everything burned.

Her breath came shallow, her hands became fists inside her pockets. He is doing it again.

Every step he took with that woman tore open another wound. Every laugh she gave him was an echo of Jane's own from years ago. She could almost see the scene unfold, how he'd found her, how he'd charmed her, how he'd start shaping her into whatever version of herself he needed.

The fear that had once paralyzed Jane all those months ago hardened into something else entirely. Something clean. Purposeful.

She followed.

They moved down the Street, the neon from a noodle shop painting their faces red as blood. Jane kept to the edge of the crowd, weaving through umbrellas, her eyes locked on the line of Stefan's shoulders. He walked like he owned the night. The woman trailed him like gravity itself pulled her in.

The wind caught her coat, and Jane thought she saw a handprint on the fabric darkened by rain or maybe something else. Her pulse quickened. Every detail felt amplified: the sound of wet shoes slapping pavement, the hum of a streetlight, the rhythm of his breathing when he leaned close to whisper something in the woman's ear.

Jane's nails dug into her palms until she felt warmth bloom there. She could not tell if it was from the rain or her own skin breaking.

They passed under a scaffolding, the city narrowing to a tunnel of rusted bars and dripping tarps. Jane matched her pace to his perfectly, every step an echo. She felt invisible, a shadow tracking another shadow.

He led the woman toward the subway entrance on the corner. The air down there would be heavy with metal and sweat. It was the kind of place Stefan loved, noise to cover his voice, darkness to hide intent. Jane's stomach knotted.

He turned suddenly, scanning the crowd.

Jane froze behind a delivery van, her breath shallow, body rigid. The rain slicked her hood, ran down her face, into her collar. Her pulse was so loud she swore it would give her away.

For a second, just a second, his gaze passed over her hiding place. Their eyes met in the reflection of a window.

She saw recognition flicker there, a ripple beneath the calm. Then he blinked and moved on, guiding the woman down the stairs.

When she stepped out from behind the van, they were gone.

She ran.

Through the crowd, through the blur of headlights and smoke. The city became a smear of motion and noise. She caught glimpses of them, his coat, her hair, then lost them again. Each turn led her deeper into the maze.

Her lungs burned. The world tilted. She shoved past people who shouted after her, but their voices did not reach her.

By the time she stopped, gasping, she was alone under the skeletal frame of the bridge. Steam rose from the grates, curling like the breath of ghosts beneath the city. The only sound was her heartbeat, hammering in her ears.

Gone.

The word echoed through her head until it became meaningless.

She pressed her palms against the cold brick wall, eyes closed, chest heaving. The rain plastered her hair to her face, blurred her vision. She was not sure if she was crying or just drenched through.

He was here. He was real.

After months of silence, months of wondering if the police were right, if she had conjured him from her own madness, he was flesh again. And he had someone new.

A spark flared inside her chest, small at first, then growing, eating the air around it. It was the same feeling she had had the night everything fell apart, the night she'd stopped being afraid and started fighting back.

That first flicker of rage that had once kept her alive now roared back, hot and steady. The fear that had once made her freeze now felt almost sweet, like fuel.

He was close.

She could find him again.

And this time, she would not run.

The city had changed temperature. Or maybe she had.

Every sound was sharper now. The passing cars hissed like snakes. The distant thunder rolled through her bones. The rain no longer felt cold, it felt like static. The air hummed with something electric.

She stood there for what could have been minutes or hours. Her reflection rippled in the puddle at her feet, fractured by raindrops. The face staring back was not frightened. It was not even angry.

It was focused.

There was no line anymore between obsession and purpose. They had become the same thing.

Jane started walking again. Not aimless this time. Her steps found rhythm. Her pulse steadied.

Every movement was calculated now. Every corner, every doorway, every reflection. She had seen him alive. She knew what he looked like now, how he moved, who he touched.

She would find him again. The city was not big enough to hide him forever.

As she walked, the old fear tried to surface again, the voice that once whispered that she was out of her depth, that she was just a broken woman chasing a ghost. But that voice was softer now, fading.

Another one was louder.

Calmer.

Colder.

You are not hunting him anymore, it said. *You are becoming what he made you to be.*

She ignored it. Or maybe she didn't.

By the time she reached her apartment, dawn had started bleeding into the sky. The windows glowed dull grey. The city exhaled steam. Jane climbed the stairs slowly, every muscle aching, her mind humming with focus.

She peeled off her wet clothes, tossed them onto the floor. The walls of her apartment seemed to pulse around her, the maps, and threads alive with energy.

She went to the board. The pins. The photos. The lines.

She drew a new circle on the map , the intersection where she had seen him. She wrote sighted beside it, then pressed her thumb over the word until it smeared.

Her pulse quickened again. It felt good. The ache in her chest had purpose now.

For months she had been drifting , a ghost searching for meaning. But now she had direction. A target.

Stefan.

She whispered his name once, but sometimes it came out wrong, Neil, Stefan or maybe her own but it did not sound like fear. It sounded like promise.

Outside, the first light crept over the rooftops, thin and grey. The city was waking up, but Jane was not tired. She had not felt this alive in months. The spark had returned, the one that had once burned her clean.

But fire did not purify. It consumed.

And she was already burning.

She stood at the window, rain streaking the glass, her reflection hovering there, Hooded hollow eyed, calm.

For the first time, she smiled.

He was out there.

He was breathing the same air.

And she was coming for him.

If she had to burn the city down to find him, she would.

Because what she once mistook for love had finally shown her its true shape.

And she was done running from it.

Now she would become it.

Chapter 6
The Pattern of Ghosts

Three days merged like water running down a fractured pane.

Jane barely remembered sleeping. She had spent the first night circling the block where she'd seen Stefan disappear, pacing between the deli and the rusted subway entrance, her pulse hammering in time with the traffic lights. Every tall man became him. Every woman's laughter sounded like that girls.

But it was not until the third morning, grey and airless, that she saw her.

The woman from that night. The one in the brown coat.

Jane spotted her leaving an apartment building, one of those narrow prewar structures with fire escapes that looked more decorative than functional. The woman had her hair tied back now, a satchel slung across her shoulder, her expression soft with the kind of tired contentment that only comes from believing you are safe.

Jane followed from across the street.

Her movements were slow, deliberate. She was no longer reacting, she was studying.

The woman walked east, cutting through the morning market. She bought a coffee from a stall by the corner, oat milk, cinnamon dusted on top. She lingered long enough to chat with the barista, a man with a shaved head who smiled at her like she was the best part of his morning. Jane filed that away: friendly, comfortable, open.

From there, the woman crossed to the kiosk on the corner, where she picked up a folded paper, The New York Times. The same paper, every morning, always from the top of the stack. She tucked it into her bag without looking at the cover. Routine. Predictable. Safe.

Jane followed her down the next block, where traffic noise softened under the weight of office chatter and delivery bikes. The woman turned down the street, pausing once to adjust her bag strap. She did not look around. Why would she?

You never expect to be prey.

Jane remembered being that woman once, the nervous glances, that ghost of unease she could never name. Stefan had been the reason all along, the shadow behind the feeling. When he finally stepped into the light, he brought safety with him, or what looked like it. It was never comfort, only control dressed as care, manipulation polished until it shone. Smoke and mirrors. Now this woman walked the same path, and Jane knew exactly what hunted her. Jane's breath misted in the cold air as she trailed her at a careful distance.

The woman's office turned out to be a boutique marketing firm tucked above a ramen bar. Jane watched her swipe a key card, push through the glass door, disappear into the elevator. The lights on the fourth floor flicked on a few minutes later. Jane stared up, watching her silhouette move across the frosted window.

She felt that same spark again, that rush of proximity. He was close.

Somewhere behind the pattern, behind this woman's gentle routines, Stefan was waiting.

Maybe he was already inside her apartment when she came home. Maybe he was watching her sleep, whispering promises against her skin. Maybe he had started the same story all over again. The thought curdled in Jane's chest like acid, the man she had loved was gone, and he was acting out the same pattern like she had never mattered at all.

She waited.

By nightfall, she'd learned the woman's name from a discarded mail package in the building's trash bins: Mara Weston. Clean handwriting, an apartment number, 4B.

The second night, Jane sat across from the building in the shadow of a lamppost, drinking bitter coffee gone cold. The fire escapes etched black lines against the pale brick, windows blinked with the blue glow of televisions.

Mara came home at 7:43. Alone. Carrying a tote of groceries. She stopped to unlock the front door, glanced up once, maybe sensing something, then went inside.

No sign of Stefan.

Jane stayed until midnight. The cold gnawed through her coat, but she barely noticed. Every sound became amplified, a window shutting above her, the scuff of boots on pavement, the faint hum of a saxophone drifting from a nearby bar.

She waited until the building went dark, until the condensation of her breath forming tiny moisture droplets on the fibres of her scarf that brushed her chin.

Then she stood.

The idea had been whispering to her since the first time she had seen the place: she needed to see inside. Needed proof that he had been there.

She crossed the street, keeping close to the wall, her pulse thrumming in her ears. The lock on the main door was old, the kind you could pick with a steady hand and a sliver of metal. She had practiced before, back when paranoia had been her only defence. She told herself this was the same thing. Research. Evidence.

Not obsession.

Never obsession.

Her fingers trembled as she slid the pick into the keyhole. Making more noise than she had intended. The rain had stopped, and the quiet pressed in like a held breath. She was halfway through the turn when a sharp voice cut the silence.

"What the hell do you think you're doing?"

Jane froze.

A flashlight beam hit her face. The landlord — wiry, late fifties, still in his nightshirt and slippers — squinted, his brow furrowing. "You shouldn't be here," he said slowly. "I've never seen you before. Who are you?"

Jane backed off instinctively, palms up, heart hammering.

"I…I dropped my keys," she stammered, the lie clumsy, her voice raw.

His eyes narrowed, hand hovering near his phone. "You don't live here, do you?"

"I…uh…i….live upstairs," Jane admitted, voice barely above a whisper.

The landlord's jaw tightened. "No you don't, get out of her before I call the cops."

Jane ran.

The flashlight bobbed behind her, his curses echoing through the narrow street. Her boots splashed through puddles as she turned the corner, ducking into an alley that smelled of rot and iron. She pressed herself against the wall, breathing hard, her pulse a drumbeat of panic.

After a minute, silence returned. Only the rain again, soft and indifferent.

Her hands shook as she pulled her hood tighter. For the first time in days, she felt something close to shame but it passed quickly. The fear turned to anger, and the anger into that old, dangerous calm.

She told herself she had been close. She had almost made it inside. Next time, she would be more careful.

The next morning, she was back.

Same corner, same hour. She watched Mara leave again, her brown coat buttoned to the throat, hair damp from the drizzle. Jane noted every movement, how she paused to check her reflection in a shop window, how she smiled at the barista, how she always tucked her left hand into her pocket as she walked.

Each action became a thread. Each thread, a map.

Jane no longer needed the pins and string on her apartment wall. The geography of Mara Weston was etched inside her head.

She learned which crosswalks she preferred, which alleys she avoided, which side of the street she hugged for cover in the rain. She even knew the pattern of lights that glowed through her window at night, bright at eight, dim by ten, out completely by eleven thirty.

A creature of rhythm. Her movements were patterned, like the beats of a song, and Jane had learned to read them. She knew it, that very predictability, clinging to routine for comfort.

It's what makes us easy prey.

But still Stefan had not appeared.

Each day that passed without him gnawed at her. It did not make sense. She had studied every story she could find, traced every thread, pieced together the faintest echoes of his movements. He *tended* to leave traces, fingerprints of manipulation, subtle shifts in behaviour—but she was missing pieces, questions that refused to answer themselves. So where was he? Was he hiding?
Or watching her, even now, laughing at the irony of it. Jane chasing a reflection of herself through the city he had built in her head?

The thought made her laugh out loud once, sharp and humourless, startling a pigeon off a ledge above her.

Maybe that was his trick. Maybe this was how he worked now, letting her do his job for him, letting her lose herself while he stayed safely in the shadows.

But that didn't matter. Because she would find him. And when she did, she would end this story before it could begin again.

On the fifth day, Jane sat on a bench near the magazine stand, pretending to read an old paper. Mara arrived at her usual time, greeting the vendor by name. Her laughter carried across the street.

Jane felt it, a strange mixture of affection and disgust. Mara was not the enemy. She was the echo. The next verse in the song. And Jane could not decide whether she wanted to save her or use her.

That realization chilled her more than the wind ever could.

She looked down at her hands, pale, cracked from the cold, faint scars glinting along her wrists where old wounds had healed. Hands like these were not meant for tenderness, they had become something else. Not for holding. Not for gentle things.

Just tools.

Just instruments.

Her coffee had gone cold. She did not notice until it spilled onto her coat.

That night, Jane sat in the alley across from Mara's building, watching the light flicker in 4B. Inside, Mara moved from room to room , a silhouette framed by curtains, phone pressed to her ear, laughter spilling into the dark.

Jane could not hear the words, but she could imagine them.

The way she had once sounded, years ago.

The softness before the storm.

Her breath fogged the glass of the empty bottle beside her. She did not blink for a long time.

He would come. He had to.

And when he did, she would be ready.

The landlord's shadow passed across the front steps at one point, a warning in human form. Jane did not flinch. She had learned where the building's blind spots were now, how to move unseen. She had learned how to wait without moving at all.

Patience was not passive. It was a weapon being honed.

And the city itself seemed to hold its breath, waiting, like her, for something to break.

By the time dawn began bleeding through the horizon again, Jane was still there. The streets were empty, washed in silver light. Her eyes burned, her muscles trembled, but her mind was razor sharp.

She knew the woman's life now , the rhythm of it, the fragile order. And somewhere inside that pattern, Stefan's shadow was waiting to appear.

Because he always did.

And this time, Jane would not lose him.

Not again.

She leaned back against the cold brick, closed her eyes, and smiled , faintly, almost tenderly.

The city felt smaller now. Closer. Like a living thing breathing with her.

All she had to do was keep watching.

Keep waiting.

The moment he stepped into the frame, she would be there.

And when that happened, the hunter and the hunted would finally occupy the same breath.

Chapter 7
The Hollow City

Three more days.

That is how long it took for sleep to become an inconvenience rather than a need.

Jane existed on caffeine, adrenaline, and the static hum of her own thoughts. She could feel the Bowery sinking into her bloodstream now, its lights, its rhythm, the endless flicker of movement that refused to let her rest.

She spent her nights in the alleys across from Mara's building, her days shadowing her through the city's routines. Each moment repeated itself like an echo through cracked glass. The more she watched, the more the pattern solidified , and the more Jane became convinced that Stefan was there, just out of sight, orchestrating everything.

Mara walked the same path to work each morning, bought the same coffee, smiled at the same people. But sometimes she hesitated midstride, a flicker of unease crossing her face. Once, she turned around suddenly on the sidewalk, eyes scanning the street. Jane had frozen in place, heart in her throat. Their eyes had not met, but Jane saw it, that creeping uncertainty she remembered from her own early days with Stefan.

That was how it started. Always small. A shiver under the skin, a whisper at the back of your neck that something was not quite right.

Jane whispered to herself as she watched, "He's getting inside her head already."

The thought made her shake. Not with fear, but something closer to anticipation.

At night, Jane's mind did not shut off. The city changed texture after midnight , the air heavier, the light too sharp. The neon bled into the fog like open wounds.

She began hearing things in the hum of the streetlights: the echo of his voice, the rhythm of his laugh. Once, while walking past a window, she thought she saw her own reflection wink at her.

The boundaries between the watcher and the watched blurred.

Sometimes she imagined herself walking up to Mara in daylight, warning her, dragging her away from the danger she did not know she was in. Other times she imagined knocking on her door and stepping inside just to feel the space where Stefan might someday stand.

By the fifth night, the idea had hardened into necessity.

She stood across the street again, half hidden behind a lamppost slick with rain. The windows of Mara's apartment were open; curtains fluttered in the weak wind. The light inside was warm, intimate. Jane could see the shadow of Mara moving around, brushing her hair, setting down a glass, pacing as if waiting for someone.

Her pulse spiked.

Was this the night?

The air seemed to hold its breath.

Jane checked her watch. Nearly midnight. She'd been there for six hours without moving. The street below was nearly empty now, save for the low rumble of a distant subway and the occasional hiss of a passing car.

When a shape turned the corner, tall, deliberate, she felt it before she saw him.

He was dressed differently this time. Black coat. Hat low. The kind of anonymity that called attention to itself. Even from across the street, she recognized the way he carried himself, shoulders loose, steps measured, the world bending slightly to his orbit.

It was him.

Her mouth went dry. Her body went still.

He stopped at the entrance to Mara's building, glanced up at her window, and something in his posture softened, affection, maybe. Or possession. It did not matter. It was the same.

The same way he used to look at her.

Jane pressed a hand against the cold metal of the lamppost to keep herself upright. Her mind flooded with images, his touch, his voice, his lies, the taste of fear and devotion that had once been indistinguishable.

He rang the buzzer. Waited.

Mara appeared in the window, surprise lighting her face. Then joy. She disappeared from view, a moment later, the front door opened, spilling warm light onto the wet street.

Jane's heart fractured.

He stepped inside, closing the door behind him. The sound of the latch was final, like a coffin seal.

For a long time, she could not move.

The night dragged on. Her body wanted to collapse, but her mind was electric. She watched the windows, waiting for movement, a shadow, a signal.

None came.

Instead, her thoughts filled the silence.

He is doing it again.

She does not even know yet.

He will drain her, just like he did to you.

Each word landed like a heartbeat.

But beneath the fury was something worse , something hollow and familiar. Jealousy.

Not because Mara had him. But because she was still inside the illusion, untouched by the truth. Jane envied the ignorance. The safety of not knowing what you were about to lose.

She whispered to herself, the words fogging the air: "You will see him for what he is. You will see."

It was not clear who she was speaking to anymore. Mara, Stefan, or her own reflection in the darkened glass.

When dawn crept in, Jane was still there. Her coat clung to her, heavy with rain. The city began to stir again, the morning routines grinding back to life.

She crossed the street just as Mara emerged from the building, face flushed, hair still damp. She looked different now, distracted, glowing, as if carrying a secret too delicate to touch.

Jane's stomach twisted.

He had been there all night.

She followed Mara through the morning crowd again, but this time the rhythm was different. The woman moved slower, smiled more easily, even hummed under her breath. The transformation had begun.

Jane kept her distance, her fingers twitching at her sides. Every gesture Mara made, every pause, every glance over her shoulder felt like déjà vu, the same choreography that had once belonged to her.

By the time Mara reached the coffee stall, Jane's pulse was ragged. The barista greeted her, said something teasing, but she barely responded. She was too far inside whatever spell he had woven overnight.

Jane turned away, unable to watch. She pressed her forehead against the cool metal of a lamppost, closing her eyes.

The city was spinning too fast.

The next two days blurred into fever.

Jane stopped eating. Her apartment became a nest of notes and photographs, the walls dense with layers of observation, times, places, fragments of overheard conversation. She wrote HE WAS THERE over and over until the pen tore through the paper.

The way she treated this map almost reminded her of a painting she tried to hard to forget, the meadow, the stream, that tree. He said it used to make him feel calm, he was so precious of it.

I used to stare at it and wish I could step inside. Now, when I dream, the stream runs red.

The city outside her window began to look different. The lights seemed brighter, but the spaces between them darker. The air buzzed with meaning she could not quite translate.

Sometimes she would catch herself smiling for no reason. Other times she would wake on the floor, unsure how long she'd been out.

But every time she closed her eyes, she saw him standing at Mara's door, the look in his eyes, calm, certain, consuming.

And every time, her breath came faster.

On the third night after his reappearance, she returned to Mara's street.

She told herself it was to confirm a suspicion. To see if he was still there.

But really, she needed proof she had not imagined it all.

The rain had stopped, leaving the streets slick and shining under the sodium lights. The city was quieter than usual, muffled, as if it too were waiting for something.

She took her place across from the building again, her old post, her pulse steady.

At 10:17 p.m., the door opened.

Stefan stepped out first. His movements were unhurried, graceful as ever. The woman followed, laughing softly, her coat slipping from her shoulders as he reached to fix it.

Jane's vision tunnelled.

The two of them walked side by side, heading east toward the main road. Mara's hand brushed his arm. He leaned down, said something that made her laugh again.

The sound was soft, familiar.

Jane followed.

Her body moved on instinct now, fluid, invisible. She stayed in the rhythm of their footsteps, matching the intervals, slipping between shadows like she had rehearsed this a thousand times.

The street narrowed ahead, funnelling them toward the subway entrance. Neon light flashed across wet pavement, reflected in puddles that looked like open eyes.

For a moment, Jane imagined she could see herself from above, a shadow trailing a pair of ghosts, all three bound by the same invisible thread.

Mara turned slightly, maybe catching movement from the corner of her eye. Jane pressed herself against the brick wall of a closed bookstore. Stefan glanced over his shoulder, quick, casual, the same habit he'd always had when sensing a gaze.

Their eyes did not meet this time. But Jane saw enough.

There was no doubt.

It was him.

The man who had destroyed her.

The man who had made her.

Her breath came out as a tremor, half sob, half laugh.

For months she had hunted his shadow. Now, finally, she had his face again , changed but unmistakable.

She whispered his name under her breath, tasting it like blood, "Stefan."

The crowd thickened near the subway steps, and she nearly lost them in the tide of bodies. Panic surged through her, wild and bright. She pushed forward, elbowing past strangers, ignoring their curses.

She reached the platform just as the train roared in, its lights slicing through the dark.

Through the window, she saw them again , Stefan and Mara, side by side, framed in the flickering fluorescent glow.

He leaned down, said something, his mouth close to her ear. Mara smiled, the expression pure and unguarded.

The doors slid shut.

Jane reached out, palm slamming against the cold metal, too late.

The train pulled away, disappearing into the tunnel's black mouth.

The air around her trembled with the echo.

She stood there long after the platform emptied, the fluorescent lights buzzing overhead.

The city hummed through her veins, every pulse aligning with its current. She felt lightheaded, exhilarated, hollow.

He was real. He was close.

And she was no longer afraid.

Something in her had shifted permanently. The part that once longed to reclaim her old life was gone, replaced by something sharper, colder.

Purpose.

She left the station and stepped back into the night, her reflection caught briefly in a shop window, eyes wide, lips parted, rain clinging to her lashes.

For a second, everything about her felt sharper, colder, deliberate. Then she smiled. The hunt was no longer about survival. It was about balance. Somewhere between predator and prey, she had found her place.

The city stretched before her, gleaming and endless. And somewhere inside it, Stefan was walking with another woman, telling the same lies, spinning the same web.

But this time, the spider was not the only thing waiting in the dark.

Chapter 8
The Shift in the Hunt

A few days folded themselves into the gutters like newspaper, damp, unreadable, thrown away. The city kept breathing around Jane as if nothing had changed: the same indifferent taxi horns, the same vendors threading coffee through steam, the same couples moving like safe islands in a river of strangers. But she had changed. The weeks of watching, the nights flat on brick with the rain seeping into her bones, had carved new channels through her mind. Those channels led to one line of thought, one blunt aim.

She tried, at first, to make the city hand him over.

For forty-eight hours she stalked the streets with a different strategy , less shadow, more signal. She left small disturbances in his likely paths, watching to see if they moved him. An opened window, a dropped glove, a cigarette stub carefully placed on a ledge outside the building. Nothing. He did not follow bait; he did not suspect, he made his own weather. The city ate everything she left like it was nothing.

Frustration thinned her patience into something honed and dangerous. If the city would not betray him, she would force the situation. She began to walk the predictable routes she had mapped, pausing at the places he had favoured, waiting for the quiet of the night to tilt the odds in her favour. She went to the jazz club where he had once lingered, sat at a corner table, and watched the door. She traced his old spots at 24hour diners, eyes on the napkin stacks and grease smudged countertops. She learned the rhythms of those rooms, the interstice between staff changeovers and the lull when people stopped noticing a face.

When that failed, when the city refused to cough him up on cue, she shifted the intent. If she could not make him come to her, she would go to where he'd already reached: Mara.

The switch felt, at first, like a small, tactical move. A different kind of proximity, closer and more controlled. It made practical sense: if he had chosen this woman, there would be threads she could tug, rituals, little repeated acts, the phone calls that always came at a certain time, the grocery runs he never noticed. If she could step into Mara's orbit quietly, invisibly, she could follow the trail back. Maybe he would follow the trail she left. Maybe he would be foolish enough to step into it.

Maybe.

Jane's apartment became a lab. The war room lit itself with a softer, crueller focus. On the board where the red thread had once crisscrossed neighbourhoods, she started pinning other things: Mara's commute times, the cafés she favoured for breakfast, the magazines she bought, the delivery schedule for the ramen bar that occupied the floor beneath her office. Each pin was a heartbeat. Each note a small incision into a life she had decided to dissect.

She rehearsed conversations in the mirror until she could deliver them without a hitch: the casual observation, the sympathetic smile, the small lie that opened doors. She learned Mara's name by saying it to herself until it stopped sounding like someone else's. Mara Weston. She tasted it like a chant. Saying it calmed and sharpened her at once.

Where she needed to be visible, she chose to be. She took to the café three blocks from Mara's office and sat with a book she never really read. She let Mara's silhouette pass by the window and logged each detail. The way she tucked hair behind an ear, how she held her coffee, the habit of checking the streetlight before crossing. Jane began to set herself gentle traps of visibility: a dropped glove that would let her make a friendly approach, an "accidental" encounter in the corridor where she would pretend to be a neighbour returning a stray pen. These were small, human things, nonthreatening, designed to make Mara lower her guard.

She told herself it was protection. It was intervention. The phrasing comforted her. It made the plan legal in her head. It let her sleep, if only in bits.

But the longer she watched, the more the lines beneath her feet started to blur. She found herself echoing Stefan's methods without noticing it: the way she watched a person's posture for clues, the soft imitation of a laugh to build trust, the careful placement of herself at the edges of someone else's life until she was part of the background. She adopted the same predatory patience that had once owned her nights. The mirror had darkened, and she did not flinch at her reflection.

Mara's life seemed ordinary to anyone who watched it from a distance. A tidy apartment in a building that smelled like lemon and old paint. A plant that, oddly, always looked healthy , watered on schedule, as if someone else made sure it did not die. Coffee orders scribbled on the same corner of her tote. Calls at the same hour. Jane memorized all these things and catalogued them like evidence. Habit by habit, she built a scaffolding around the woman.

She tried one contact. At the dentist's office where she had once had a chipped incisor fixed, Jane found the receptionist and spoke to her, mentioned she had met a woman named mara here a few times and was meant to join her somewhere at the weekend if she was free but jane mentioned she couldn't recall exactly, the receptionist mentioned Mara's volunteer work on weekends. Small anchoring points. The receptionist gave names, parks where Mara sometimes ran, a community art class she taught on Thursday evenings. Jane went to the class under the pretence of interest in watercolours. She stood at the back, anonymous, watching Mara lead a group with soft authority. The woman's hands moved with quiet confidence over paper and pigment. No sign of Stefan. No sign of anything other than gentleness.

It hurt to watch. Not the gentle part, she had once been that gentleness, but the ease with which Mara existed within a world that had no idea how delicate she had become. Jane reminded herself that gentleness was a beacon for predators.

She began to push the boundaries. Nothing overt, no threats, no confrontations. Small probes: a missed appointment she made sure to be seen at near Mara's building, a delivery that arrived with the wrong name but right floor, a casual passing compliment that let Mara reward her with a smile but was fleeting enough that Mara did not get to learn Janes face in too much detail. Each interaction left Jane's skin buzzing with a light that felt dangerously like hope.

On the nights she could not sleep she sketched scenarios on the back of old receipts, the ink smeared from her shaking hands. Her handwriting, once clean and practical, grew angular and precise: room layouts, escape vectors, timing estimates scribbled in the margins. The sketches were fantasies, violent, direct but never technical. They stopped before the vital details, like a dream that faded at the border between the waking and the imagined. She was careful not to make an instruction manual of her rage. Even in the dark, her conscience or what remained of it kept the how's under a tight lid. Instead, she filled the page with the why: words strung together in acid clarity.

Why did you do it?

Why did you make this?

Why did you choose softness to hunt?

The questions roared louder than any plan.

At times she found herself listening for the man she hated even when she had no reason to. In the elevator of a laundry, in line for a sandwich, in the lull at a crosswalk, she had let her gaze rove, searching for the architecture of his gait. Once, across three lanes of traffic, she saw a profile that could have been his. Her stomach flipped and then calmed as she watched him disappear inside a bar. She walked past the doorway with the deliberate economy of someone who was practicing restraint and whispered into the rain, not yet.

A curious thing happened in those days: she started to dream in rooms. Not the real rooms she crept through, but the ones she imagined. In the dreams, she saw him strapped to something, bound, uncomprehending, finally human. It was not violent in the cinematic sense; it was a question waiting to be asked. She rehearsed the questions: the slow, cold tones she imagined would force the truth out of him. Why? Why us? Was it enjoyment or hunger? The rehearsals were not mechanical. They were interrogation as confession; she imagined the answers as a map out of her own ruin.

After one such dream, she woke with her palm pressed to the map's edge, the paper damp with sweat. The thought of questioning him in a room, looking at his eyes and making him acknowledge what he'd done, was less about justice than about the order of things. She wanted a line drawn through the chaos, a ledger balanced.

Still, she would not, could not, write the details of restraint. The mind drew a line there, as if to keep a sanctum of humanity. Perhaps that was what remained of her: the last human refusal to become purely instrumental. She kept her plans fuzzy in the corners. In her dark, she told herself the clarity would come in the moment; that questions could be tools without making her into a blueprint for brutality.

One night, walking home after an unsuccessful attempt to intercept a delivery she thought might be tied to him, she watched Mara from across the street as the woman unlocked her door. A small maintenance truck idled nearby, men folded maps and cigarette smoke into their hands. Mara paused to pick up a flyer someone had stuck into the metal railing, a community notice about a neighbourhood cleanup. She crumpled it politely and tossed it into a bin. A face from the past flickered in Jane's mind: the face of her own obedient compliance before everything fell apart.

She realized, then, that this was no longer only about finding him. The hunt had redrawn the horizon of herself; she was not merely pulling on threads to reach Stefan. She was, little by little, knotting those threads into a net around someone who had not yet done anything wrong, someone whose life was only a sequence of tiny, ordinary moments.

A low, slow warning sound rose in the back of her mind, an animal's hiss, every time she reached that realization. But the warning felt like a separate voice, one that she could observe now rather than obey. She catalogued it, stored it, and moved on.

She began, tentatively, to plan more concrete things. Safe rooms she could use as waiting places. Places with no cameras and exits. Neighbours who never noticed patterns, perfect blanks for staging an accidental encounter. She marked them on the map with a different colour, softer, almost tentative, as if the colour itself could keep the schematic from hardening into a blueprint.

Evenings blurred into a cadence of preparation. She busied herself with logistics and rehearsals that never grew precise enough to become real. The restraint was part calculated caution and part secret mercy. She wanted him to be questioned. She wanted answers like a medicine. She imagined him small and quelled, the monstrous architecture of his charm exposed and helpless. She imagined herself not triumphant but unmade by the truth, because she believed that if she could make him name what he did, the world might make sense again.

But the more she planned, the more the line she had been guarding thinned.

There was a thrum in the city that said she was close. Every smell, every echo put him nearer. Yet the closeness had a cost she could taste: a softening at the edges of her own mind, small echoes of his calm settling where her fear used to live. Her empathy had been repurposed into a tool. Her rage had been trimmed into focus.

She told herself the change was necessary. That it was part of the trade off for making pain pay. That she would be different at the end. Better, perhaps. Cleaner. Safer.

In the nights that followed, as the city settled into its small, forgetful rhythms, Jane would sit before the map and let her fingers hover above the pins. The plan sat there at the edge of thought, half conceived, half denied, a hunger for truth wrapped in the language of restraint. She did not yet know how she would bring him into a room and make him speak. She only knew she wanted it and that everything she did now was a preface to that demand.

Inside, the boards of her apartment groaned with the weight of intent. Somewhere between the map and the quiet, she felt the shape of something terrible forming, soft at first, then hardening like glass in a kiln.

She folded the paper over and wrote one word beneath the cluster of pins, a promise to herself that read less like a plan than like a vow. Soon.

Chapter 9
The Leverage

Jane had stopped thinking in linear days. Hours were more precise moments bracketed by Mara's movements, the exact sequence of steps that carried her to the office, the café, the grocery, and back. Each repeated action was a promise Jane made to herself: a promise that if she learned the rhythm, she could bend it, twist it, and use it to pull Stefan out into the open.

She followed Mara the morning after the last near encounter, keeping her distance but allowing visibility. A café window provided a vantage point across the street; Jane sat in shadow, sipping coffee she barely tasted. Mara's brown coat had shifted slightly with the weather. The woman laughed at the barista's joke, tilted her head, and brushed a strand of hair behind her ear. Every detail, every micro expression, was logged in Jane's mind.

She began weaving herself into Mara's life in invisible threads. A mislaid pen "found" in the office hallway. A package accidentally left at the wrong apartment door, which Jane returned at the precise moment Mara passed by. A brief exchange in the elevator: casual, polite, quick, inconsequential. Each gesture was small, but it reinforced a presence, a ghost she could follow without suspicion.

Jane never smiled. Her energy was neutral, fluid, professional. She practiced the subtle manipulations with a precision that startled even her. It was a delicate dance, close enough to be seen, distant enough to remain unknowable. She watched Mara notice her occasionally, an eyebrow flick, a polite nod, and Jane allowed herself a tiny thrill. Influence was intoxicating. She could feel Stefan's methods sliding into her veins, the patience, the timing, the subtle shaping of perception.

By the third day, Jane had tracked Mara to a small art supply shop. Mara asked the clerk for a specific brush, the same kind she had purchased the previous week. Jane lingered nearby, watching the exchange, noting the pattern, the predictability, the innocence.

When Mara left, she paused outside to check her phone, and Jane stepped closer. Not too close, careful, invisible, but close enough to hear her mutter: "I should probably get started on the class tomorrow." The voice was light, soft, ordinary. And yet it carried a fragility Jane could exploit.

She began shadowing Mara more aggressively, attending a yoga class, pretending to browse the same aisle in the grocery. Jane did not want Mara to notice her. She wanted Mara to trust her presence, to accept it as a harmless constant.

At night, Jane poured over maps, over the sequences she had recorded in her journal. She noted where Mara bought groceries, which crosswalks she used, the benches she favoured when waiting for her morning coffee. Jane even started cataloguing the faintest habits, the way Mara rotated her bag strap from one shoulder to another, the time she always lingered at the corner before entering her building. Everything could be leveraged, everything was data.

And through it all, Stefan's shadow haunted her. Every time Mara's routines placed her in proximity to a place Stefan might pass, Jane's pulse spiked. She imagined him watching, smirking from some darkened doorway, testing the predator in her.

It was a game now. A hunt in reverse. She had learned from the master. And she was becoming something that no one could stop, least of all herself.

The tension ratcheted the night Mara hosted her art class. Jane arrived early, posing as a student interested in watercolours. She watched Mara prepare the studio: brushes lined up, paints squeezed into neat wells, aprons folded on the backs of chairs. Mara's voice, clear and soft, guided the attendees as they dipped into pigment and water. Jane memorized every subtlety, the tilt of her head, the gentleness of her corrections, the patience in her tone.

She lingered in the back, pretending to concentrate on her own canvas, but her attention was a laser beam. She began to imagine ways to isolate Mara, to influence her actions subtly, to push her toward making decisions that would allow Jane to finally intersect with Stefan's orbit directly.

A trivial detail became a leverage point: Mara's habit of leaving her front door slightly ajar when returning late at night. She had noted the time, 11:37 p.m., every night this week. A vulnerability Jane could exploit.

The class ended, and Mara gathered her things. Jane stayed, "helping" with small tasks, stacking chairs, folding aprons, sweeping the floor. Mara thanked her softly, barely registering her presence. Jane stored the smile, the small acknowledgment, in her mind like a card in a hand she had not yet played.

Outside, the streets were slick with rain. Jane shadowed Mara at a measured distance as she walked toward her apartment, making careful notes of the route, the alternate alleys, the dim streetlights. Stefan did not appear, but Jane didn't need him to. This was part of the plan: she was building a web of influence, testing the limits, waiting for him to emerge.

And then, for the first time in days, Jane felt a surge of the old clarity. The spark that had once set her obsession aflame, the one that had first transformed fear into purpose, reignited. She did not need to see Stefan to know he was near. The rhythm of her stalking, the discipline of her patience, the slow, quiet shaping of Mara's routines, it was all a signal that she was drawing closer to him, and closer to the monster she feared she was becoming.

She let herself smile briefly, savouring the sensation. The city was hers to watch, to influence, to manipulate. And soon, she thought, the two of them would be in her crosshairs, whether they knew it or not.

But the night ended with a near miss.

A black sedan glided along the street as Mara reached her building. Jane froze behind the corner of a shop. The car slowed, a door opened, and a figure stepped out, tall, deliberate. Stefan. Only he did not see her. He followed Mara's steps closely, offering a hand, a whispered word, a smile she could not see but imagined perfectly. Jane's stomach knotted, a mixture of triumph and frustration. She had been so close, too close to make the interception, to catching him in a small misstep, and yet the city swallowed him, blending him into the night as if he'd never been there.

Jane's hands curled into fists. She did not cry. She did not breathe deeply. She only waited, her patience sharp, her mind already recalculating. The spark roared again: not just the need to find him, but the need to control the narrative.

She slipped into the shadows, following Mara and Stefan with renewed purpose, knowing that every step brought her closer to the inevitable confrontation.

Chapter 10
The Convergence

Three nights later, Jane had everything she needed.

She had tracked Mara's habits to near perfection. She had studied the alternate routes, the times she left and returned, the slight vulnerabilities Stefan could exploit, if she allowed herself to see them as such. But Jane had no intention of allowing him that control. She was no longer content to be the ghost in the corner, the shadow waiting for him to make a move. The time had come to switch tactics.

Mara had been her lever. Stefan's absence from the streets was a puzzle. Jane's mind, restless and electric, decided the answer, make him reveal himself, draw him out, force his presence into a space she controlled.

She found a small, abandoned space on the periphery of Mara's neighbourhood, one with a door that clicked solidly, blinds that closed tightly, and no one living above. She spent the day assembling the room: two sturdy chairs found in the space, ropes coiled neatly on the floor she had picked up that day and a small table in the centre. The space was minimal but sufficient, functional. Neutral. Perfect for forcing confrontation.

But first, she had to get him in.

She watched Mara as she left her apartment for the market. Jane shadowed her at a careful distance, whispering into her ear that she was merely a concerned neighbour, a helpful presence, a shadow that might be invisible but was always nearby. Mara walked with her habitual grace, unaware that Jane had been weaving her path around hers for weeks.

The night had finally come.

Mara returned home, weary from the day, arms heavy with groceries and the dull weight of routine. Jane had been waiting, weeks of planning, of patience so taut it hummed beneath her skin. Now, every motion was measured. Calculated.

A stumble on the stairwell carefully staged, something small left where a careless foot might catch, elegantly clumsy . Jane was there to catch her, the picture of concern. Apologies. Small talk. An easy offer of help.

And just like that, Mara led Jane into her apartment, unaware that's exactly where Jane had meant to end up .

The door clicked shut, soft as a whisper. Street noise vanished. Silence became a presence of its own.

Jane stood within Mara's world now. If her timing was right, Stefan would be here soon, the man who had tried to kill her, who had buried her once and left her to die.

All she had to do was wait.

She let Mara start talking, Mara apologised for her hastiness, she was expecting someone. Jane knew exactly who she meant, her heart started to race but Jane calmed herself down. Now is not the time to let fear, impatience or rage set in. all this time leading to this moment, Jane reminded herself to stay calm and she did, she let Mara continue mundane chatter about art classes and deadlines, replying softly, keeping answers short and calculated but her eyes clinical.

Mara mentioned a name, a name Jane had not known but the feeling in her chest told her enough when she heard the name John slip Mara's Mouth with a loving and naïve tone.

She could ask Mara. She wanted to ask Mara, just one question, just to see if Mara would open up, see if she would give up Stefans new mask in its entirety.

The thought kept coming to her, quick and intrusive, the way a shard of glass catches light. A simple question here, a gentle prod there, nothing that would ring alarms. Mara was open, soft, the kind of woman who mistook politeness for safety.

But every time Jane imagined forming the words, something in her chest constricted. It felt reckless. Loud. Asking anything at all would mean stepping out of the quiet orbit she'd built around the woman, breaking the fragile veil that kept Jane invisible and harmless. One misplaced question and Mara would stiffen, or falter.

Besides, what could Mara give her? Fragments. Misunderstandings. Whatever version of Stefan she'd been fed. Jane didn't need another woman's confusion; she carried enough of her own to drown in.

And why interrogate the echo when the source was drawing closer by the hour? Stefan was somewhere inside this tightening loop. The city felt different now, charged, as if every shadow hummed with the shape of him. Jane wouldn't risk her plan for a scrap of information she'd rip straight from his mouth soon enough. Face-to-face. Eye-to-eye.

Still… the urge tugged at her. A thin, sharp whisper. Ask. Push. Break the surface.

If Jane pushed too hard, if she looked too curious, Mara would feel it. She'd flinch. She'd remember the shape of Jane's face. And people who remembered became liabilities, became obstacles.

One wrong question could ruin everything. She couldn't afford obstacles, not now, not when she has come so close.

Jane exhaled slowly, letting the impulse burn out in her throat.

Patience had carved her into the creature she had become. Impulse had buried her once already.

She would not let it happen again.

Jane's mind ticked like a metronome. She didn't want to hurt Mara. The girl was just another piece on the board, a pawn she was saving by using. That's what she told herself, anyway.

If Jane pushed too hard, if she looked too curious, Mara would feel it. She'd flinch. She'd remember the shape of Jane's face. And people who remembered became liabilities.

One wrong question could ruin everything.

So she stayed quiet. Watching. Waiting. Letting the urge burn itself out in her throat.

When Mara turned her back to put the groceries away, Jane acted. She slipped a sleeping pill from her pocket — one of the many doctors had prescribed rather than deal with the real issue.

A faint crack of a capsule. A swirl in the wine glass.

Harmless. Efficient.

Now wait.

They had moved their small talk to the living room and from the corner, Jane watched. Her pulse beat steady, then faster. Adrenaline blurred with something else, something dark and electric. When Mara's eyelids fluttered, she began to sink deeper into the sofa then eventually into sleep midsentence, Jane exhaled, quiet and controlled.

The first piece had fallen.

Now came the real test.

She checked her watch.

Almost time.

He would come, he always did, drawn by the same predictable hunger. When Stefan stepped through that door, he would expect Mara. He would find something else entirely.

Jane slipped into the shadows, heart steady, mind cold. Not too much time went by when the hinges creaked.

Footsteps.

Then, his voice, low, familiar, careless. Calling Mara's name.

He took one step too far into the room.

And then Jane sprang into action with the precision of a guillotine and the certainty of fate.

Chapter 11
The Inversion

Stefan woke to a darkness so complete it seemed to press against his skin. The smell was faintly metallic, tinged with dust and something warmer, something that made his stomach tighten. He tried to move, felt the slick press of a surface against his wrists and ankles, and realized he was not sitting on a bed or a sofa. He was not sitting anywhere he had known. He was restrained.

A faint awareness and familiarity crawled through him, a chill at the edge of his mind, someone else had set the stage. Someone who understood him better than he thought anyone could.

Panic rippled through him first in sharp stabs, then in long, crawling waves. His chest tightened. The faint light spilling through a single cracked window revealed just enough: a chair across from him, its occupant slumped forward as though sleeping or unconscious.

"Mara?" His voice cracked. The sound seemed foreign in the darkness, unfamiliar even to himself. "Mara! Are you okay?"

No answer.

He tried to push himself upright. The ropes cut into his wrists, biting, pulling. They were tied expertly tight, unyielding, designed to frustrate without immediate pain. His legs were anchored in the same way. Heart hammering,

Stefan wriggled, tugged, kicked. The more he struggled, the more impossible it became. He was trapped.

He leaned forward, peering across the small, shadowed room. The figure in the chair didn't move. A sense of dread began to gnaw at him. The angles were wrong. The posture was wrong. The weight on the chair… too familiar, this situation all too familiar.

He inhaled sharply. The chair creaked slightly under the weight of the person slumped in it. He had been certain it was Mara. Who else could it be? But something felt wrong. He had lured her in , had orchestrated the delicate moments that made her obey and isolate around him. He had anticipated her fear, her reactions. She would have struggled. She would have protested. She would have looked at him with terrified understanding. But he had not orchestrated this. Not this time.

The chair shifted. The figure lifted slightly, a slow, deliberate movement. Stefan's stomach dropped.

And then came the sound that froze the blood in his veins, a laugh.

Soft at first, then louder, darker, curling through the shadows. A laugh that he knew. The kind that carried both amusement and malice.

Stefan's eyes widened. He tried to speak again. "Mara…?"

"Not quite," came the voice, low, measured, venom wrapped in silk.

The figure lifted fully now, straightening into the chair. The light that had obscured the figure now caught her face just enough for him to recognize her. The black of her hair, the ashen pallor, the eyes that had once burned with fear now glittering with something far more dangerous, mastery.

Jane.

Stefan's jaw dropped. His mind scrambled, cogs turning too fast. "Jane? What… what is this? What have you done? You are supposed to be dead?" "The News, they reported you dead….how are you…why are you…"

She leaned back slightly, letting the ropes around her own wrists and ankles slacken just enough to suggest a false helplessness, a mirror of his own deception. The chair creaked under her, a calculated accent to her posture. "Done?" she repeated, letting the word linger. "I think you mean… what have I finally done with you."

Stefan swallowed, forcing calm into his voice.

"Jane… look at me."

His tone softened, almost gentle.

"Whatever this is, we can figure it out. We always did, remember?"

He leaned forward slightly, searching her face, he forced a smile.

"You don't have to do this. We can get through it together."

Jane laughed softly.

"There it is."

She leaned forward, eyes gleaming.

"The voice. The calm one you used when you wanted people to trust you."

Her smile sharpened. She studied him for just a moment. "You really thought that would still work on me?"

Stefan's expression flickered, just for a moment then the panic rose. He thrashed in the ropes, tugging harder. The knots held. He could barely breathe through the panic clawing at his chest. "You can't, this is impossible! I've, Mara… you've… she…"

Jane tilted her head, a slow, measured gesture that mirrored the faintly theatrical cruelty Stefan himself had once enjoyed. She chuckled, low and controlled at first, then sharper, more vicious. "You've always assumed," she said, "that you were untouchable. That your charm, your arrogance, your little games could bend anyone to your will. Even me." "Don't worry about Mara, she is safe now, she is still sleeping in her apartment".

Stefan's eyes narrowed. Confusion warred with disbelief, then horror. "I… you can't… you think,"

Jane laughed again, louder this time, the sound filling the small room. "I stopped guessing months ago, Stefan. I started learning. You are predictable. Arrogant. Fragile under pressure. Every little game you have played… I have learned to play better. And now, here you are, in *my* trap, not yours..."

Jane's smile widened slightly.

"You spent years learning how to hunt people, Stefan." She tilted her head, studying him like a specimen.

"You never imagined one of them might learn how to hunt you back."

He struggled harder, but the ropes only dug deeper into his wrists. The chair's legs scraped against the floor as he twisted, tried to leverage himself free.

"You're insane!" he spat. His voice was sharp, trembling with fury and fear. "This isn't you. This isn't…"

Jane leaned forward, her eyes glinting in the faint light. "Isn't me?" she whispered. "Oh, Stefan… this is exactly me. The one you created when you tore everything apart. Do you remember fear? Do you remember the nights you spent orchestrating it in others? The trembling faces, the small, silent screams?"

Stefan froze. Her words, precise and deliberate, hit him like a series of blows. He had never imagined herself mastering this… this complete domination of both mind and body.

Jane continued, letting the words drip like poison. "You thought you could take everything, control everyone, leave no trace. But you left one mistake… one person who remembered the map of your cruelty. And I've been tracing it back ever since. Every lie, every manipulation, every soft little victim you thought was yours to use, remember Emily? Remember me? Remember how it felt to believe in something you would never give back?"

Stefan's breathing quickened, his panic sharpening into real fear. He could feel the trap closing around him, not physical, but psychological. Jane had studied him, mirrored him, anticipated him. The irony cut deeper than any blade.

She leaned back again, slumping slightly in the chair, the picture of casual dominance. "I could have killed you. I could have made this the end. But I want… I want to see you squirm first. I want you to understand what it feels like to be in my hands."

Stefan's mind raced. The situation defied him, he had no vantage, no leverage, no game to play. He looked around, searching for a weapon, a weak point in the room. The walls were bare, the light dim, the air thick with Jane's presence.

Her laugh came again, echoing off the concrete and brick. Not the playful laugh he'd once toyed with, but the cruel, knowing, sharpened laugh of someone who had crossed the line between victim and predator.

"Look at you," she said softly, almost kindly, but the venom underlined it. "You always assumed you'd leave a trail of broken lives and walk away untouched. Now? Now the roles are… let's just say… redistributed."

Stefan struggled again, the panic rising to raw terror. "You, this isn't real. This can't be real. You can't…"

Jane tilted her head again, savouring the rise and fall of his chest, the tremor in his fingers. "Oh, it's real, Stefan. You should know by now. I watched you, I watched Mara. I waited. I learned. And now, finally… here we are."

She let the words hang in the air, sharp and heavy, letting him stew in his helplessness. The ropes cut into his skin with every subtle movement, but the real torment was psychological. He had no control, no foresight, and no ally. She had stripped him of the arrogance he had relied on for so long.

"Do you feel it?" she whispered, leaning closer. "The shift? The understanding? For once, it is not about fear… it is about inevitability. Every little thing you did to others… it is reflected right back at you. I have spent months learning you, anticipating you, bending the world quietly until the moment I could make it mine. And now, Stefan… it is mine."

The light caught her face as she leaned back again, a slow, satisfied grin spreading across her features. His panic mingled with confusion, disbelief, and a creeping, suffocating terror. He realized, finally, that he had no escape. Not from her, not from this room, not from the slow, deliberate unravelling of his control.

Jane laughed one final time, the sound a cruel music in the darkness, echoing off the walls, reminding him of every manipulation he had ever inflicted. Her eyes glimmered with triumph and cruelty, but beneath it all was the quiet, terrifying calm of someone who had claimed power utterly.

And for the first time, Stefan realized he was not the most dangerous person in the room, he was truly trapped, not just in the ropes, not just in the room, but in the game, one he had never imagined losing.

Jane slumped back in her chair again, allowing the dim light to catch the angle of her jaw, the sharpened edges of her gaze, the faint traces of sleepless nights and relentless obsession that had brought her here.

The room was still. The trap complete. The predator finally contained.

And for once, she was the one laughing.

Chapter 12
The Reckoning

The room was small, oppressive, lit only by a single weak lamp in the corner. Shadows clung to the walls, stretching and twisting the furniture into monstrous silhouettes. The air itself was heavy , carrying every breath like a confession he didn't want to make.

Stefan's wrists burned against the ropes, his body rigid, every muscle fighting restraint. But it wasn't the rope that terrified him. The real terror came from what he did not know: the woman across from him was no longer the trembling victim he remembered. She was patient, deliberate, and terrifyingly calm. Every movement, every blink, every micro expression was carefully measured.

Jane leaned forward, elbows on her knees, fingers laced. Her expression was still, unreadable , the kind of stillness that makes people confess without realizing why. Stefan's eyes darted over her face, seeking mercy, searching for weakness, any flicker of humanity to cling to. There was none.

"There's a tree," she said, voice low, deliberate. "A particular one. Do you remember it?"

Stefan's brow furrowed, a subtle flinch betraying him. "I… I don't know what you mean."

Jane's lips curved into a faint, humourless smile. "You do. The tree where you buried Emily. Where you thought you buried the truth. It mattered to you. It always did."

"How do you…" His breath faltered.

"I know," she said simply. "I have been watching. Listening. You leave traces, Stefan. Even when you think you are clean."

He shifted, the ropes cutting into his wrists. "You think this changes anything?"

Jane shook her head slowly. "It changes everything. You spent your life sculpting fear into something beautiful. Now it is time you look at the sculpture you built."

"It's just a tree," he said, forcing composure that did not fit his trembling voice.

The silence that followed was absolute , a vacuum that pulled the truth out of him. The lamplight flickered, fractured shadows dancing across his face. Jane waited. She did not push. She did not need to.

Finally, he exhaled.

"It all started at that tree," he said.

Jane's expression remained still. She just listened.

"My brother and I… we used to play there every day after school, every summer morning. Climb it, race to the top, scrape our knees, laugh like the world stopped for us," he said, voice fragile. "It was ours. The bark was smooth, the branches wide enough to hold anything we could imagine. The air smelled of sap and sunlight. I felt… alive there. Safe. Connected. He was my world, my compass."

He looked away, his hands trembling. "Until the day it didn't."

Jane's voice was almost a whisper. "He fell?"

Stefan nodded slowly, his eyes glassy. "We climbed too high. It had rained the night before. The bark was slick. He reached for a branch, it snapped, and he… he fell." His breath hitched. "The sound, the thud, the silence… I remember thinking how still he looked. How peaceful. And for one terrible second… I felt something else. Something dark. A thrill I didn't understand. Excitement. Chaos. Power."

The confession hung between them, obscene and raw.

"I didn't understand it," he continued, voice low. "That rush, that chaos… when my parents found out, when they looked at me, when they stopped seeing me as their son… I became a ghost. A shadow. I tried to reach them, tried to call their attention, tried to be the boy they loved. But I couldn't. Their eyes said everything: you are the reminder, the mistake that survived."

He laughed once, hollow, bitter. "They didn't hit me. They didn't yell. They just… stopped existing in my life. I would walk into a room, and the air thickened. Their love was gone, replaced by silence. Their indifference was punishment enough."

He paused, rubbing at his wrists. "I started sneaking back to the tree at night. Touching the earth where he had fallen. Sometimes… it felt warm. Almost alive. Like it remembered him. Like it understood what had happened. That's where the darkness first whispered to me. It told me I was chosen for something else. That I could see truths others were too weak to face. That beauty always rots underneath, and those endings… endings are pure."

He met Jane's gaze. "You think darkness just arrives, Jane? It doesn't. It grows. It watches. It learns your name.

It waits until you need it most. And then… it devours you slowly, until the line between fear and pleasure, control and chaos, is gone."

The lamp flickered, faint and sickly. Jane did not flinch.

"Then came Emily," he said, softer, almost reverent, as if speaking her name aloud could shatter him. "She was light. She looked at me like I wasn't broken. She didn't see the darkness in me… or maybe she did, and thought she could fix it. For a while, I believed I could be… human again. Loved. Safe."

His shoulders sagged. "But light doesn't stay. It burns. And when she started to pull away, when she stopped looking at me like I mattered… the darkness came back. Hungrier this time. Whispering that if I didn't control her, I'd lose her. That if I lost her, I'd never matter again. I tried to hold on tighter, to cage it, to bury it beneath her laughter, beneath the memory of us. But it was too late. I snapped."

His voice cracked. "I took her to the tree. Familiar. Beautiful… but rotten underneath. I buried her there, thinking maybe if I hid her beneath it, the darkness would sleep. It didn't."

He closed his eyes. "That's when I took his name , my brother's. Stefan died with him. If I becamc someone else, maybe I could start over. Maybe the dark would forget me."

Jane tilted her head, voice calm, precise. "And it never left, did it?"

He looked up, hollow. "You tell me. Because when I saw you, I thought maybe this time would be different. But the darkness… saw you first."

The silence was unbearable , for him, not for her.

Stefan strained against the ropes. "You can't do this, this isn't justice!"

"Justice?" she said, voice detached. "No, Stefan. This is understanding. Tonight, you will know what it is like to be the one unmade."

The room seemed to shrink. The shadows pressed closer. Jane's eyes gleamed in the flickering light, patient, unblinking.

For the first time, Stefan truly understood what it meant to lose control.

Jane's laughter was soft, almost melodic, echoing faintly off the concrete walls. It was not joy. It was release, cold and surgical. The echo lingered long after she stopped, curling around him like smoke.

He sat there, trembling, a man dissected by his own truth. And Jane, slumped back in her chair, allowed herself the smallest, sharpest smile.

Victory was a slow burn. And she had stoked it to perfection.

The lamp buzzed once more. The shadows deepened. And in that dim, airless room , between confession and consequence , the balance finally shifted.

Jane rose slowly, letting the shadow of her body stretch across the floor like an omen. "You've carried that all this time," she said evenly. "The fall. The girl. The graves. And you sit there, and You think the truth redeems you?"

Stefan shook his head, voice broken. "No. I just… I thought maybe it would make sense to someone."

"It doesn't," Jane said, letting the words hang, final, almost ceremonial.

His chest heaved. Every instinct, every carefully honed tactic, every plan he had ever executed, useless. Jane had mapped it all, mirrored it, absorbed it, and turned it against him.

The lamp flickered again, casting fractured shadows across his face. Jane leaned back slightly, letting him stew in the helplessness he had never known. He tried to plan, to speak, to manipulate but the room swallowed every attempt. The ropes held. The shadows watched. And the faint glint of steel on the edge of the lamp caught his eye: a knife, thin and deliberate, hovering just in his peripheral vision.

Stefan's chest rose and fell erratically. Panic flared. He jerked against the ropes. Jane did not flinch. She did not speak. She simply existed, patient, calm, meticulous. Every moment was deliberate, every second stretched until it was unbearable.

"You feel it?" she whispered, letting the words crawl along the air like smoke. "The helplessness? The fear? The understanding that every assumption you made… every arrogance you wielded… is meaningless?"

"Yes," he breathed, trembling. "I… I see it. I… understand."

Jane's smile was faint, almost imperceptible, but sharp. "Good. That is only the beginning. The beginning of reckoning. The beginning of everything you thought you could control… unravelling."

Stefan's mind raced. His past, his trauma, his obsession, his darkness everything he had buried, was laid bare. He could not escape it. He could not fight it. He understood the depth of the predator's fall: he was entirely, painfully… powerless.

And Jane, slumped back, the half light catching just the corner of her mouth, allowed herself the smallest, sharpest smile. Victory was a slow burn. She had stoked the flames perfectly. The balance had shifted. The predator had become the prey.

The room was silent except for the faint creak of the ropes and the low, uneven thrum of two heartbeats. Jane's eyes flicked briefly toward the window, just the edge of her vision catching the storm's restless movement outside. Was it a trick of light, a shadow, or simply rain? She did not know. And yet, it felt as if the room itself held its breath with her.

She leaned back further, letting the shadows stretch across the floor, her presence filling the air like a slow pulse. Somewhere between heartbeat and silence, between control and collapse, the first stirrings of something new awakened within her, quiet, deliberate, patient, and hungry.

The lamp buzzed faintly. And in that dim, airless room between confession and consequence, between shadow and self, the balance had quietly and irrevocably shifted.

Chapter 13
Silence Between Heartbeats

Silence had a weight. It pressed against the walls, heavy and suffocating, like the world had shrunk to this single, breathing space. The lamp flickered once, twice, before its weak glow steadied, casting long, uncertain shadows across the corners of the room. Jane sat opposite Stefan, the knife in her hand. The metal glimmered faintly, almost alive in the dim light.

For a moment, she thought she heard movement outside, a whisper against the glass, a shuffle that could have been rain or breath, but the lamp buzzed again, and the world folded inward.

Stefan's chest rose and fell rapidly, the ropes biting into his skin, a physical reminder of his powerlessness, but it wasn't the physical restraint that held him. The terror clinging to his eyes was sharper, rawer, and in it, Jane could read every calculation, every flicker of instinct he had spent a lifetime honing. And she had anticipated all of it.

"You know," Jane said softly, her voice low and deliberate, "I never thought I'd find myself here. Doing exactly what you did to me."

Stefan's eyes widened, disbelief cracking his voice. "You… you're the one in control. You can stop…"

Jane's lips curved into a faint, almost predatory smile. "Control?" she echoed, tilting her head. "Look at me, Stefan. Look at how I watch you. The way I anticipate every flinch, every breath, every twitch. You feel it, don't you? That pressure? That tightness in your chest? That's control. That's what I've felt for months, tracing you, studying you. Only now, it's me you feel."

He tried to twist, jerk, but the ropes held firm. Panic sharpened his voice. "You… this isn't… you! This is madness! You're… insane!"

Jane leaned forward slightly, letting the shadows stretch across her face. "Insane?" she murmured. "Or… awakened. The Jane you knew is dead, you succeeded with that at least. The girl you said loved, the girl you wanted to keep… to shape….to break….she's gone. And in her place… something else lives now. Calculating. Ruthless. Patient. Hungry. Just like you."

The words seemed to echo in the small room, settling over him like dust. Stefan's mind raced. He had always understood fear, always controlled panic. But this… this was different. This was intimate, invasive, precise. Jane wasn't just matching him; she had transcended him.

"You killed Emily," Jane said softly, almost conversationally. "You buried her beneath that tree. Your tree. You thought you could hide everything, bury the guilt, bury the darkness. And you thought it would make you clean. Perfect. Untouchable."

Stefan's eyes flickered, a sudden flash of fear mingled with denial. "You… you don't understand! You can't! You…"

Jane cut him off with a tilt of her head, letting silence press against him. She let the words sit between them, heavy and accusing. Then, slower, almost a whisper.

"I understand perfectly. Every obsession. Every fear. Every manipulation. Every small cruelty. Every life you touched, you shaped, you controlled… I learned it. I traced it back heartbeat by heartbeat until I could anticipate you better than you could anticipate yourself. And now… you feel it. You're tasting it. Powerless. Exposed. Helpless. Just like I was."

Stefan's chest heaved. His mind scrambled, trying to find leverage, a flaw, a mistake, anything but there was none. Jane's calm was an armour, impenetrable.

Jane leaned closer, letting her eyes glint in the faint lamp glow. "Do you feel it?" she whispered. "The helplessness? The knowledge that all your careful patterns, every instinct you've honed… meaningless. That arrogance, that precious confidence… gone."

His panic surged. "You… you can't… I won't… you're insane,"

Jane held up a hand. "Quiet," she said softly. "Listen."

At first, he heard only the scrape of the ropes and the distant hum of the lamp. Then soft, faint, the sound of his own heartbeat. Rapid, erratic. Panic-stricken. And beneath it… another. A slower pulse, deliberate, echoing through the room like a drum he couldn't escape.

"You hear it?" Jane murmured. "Two hearts. One room. One life taken. One life… unrecognizable. Mine and yours, Stefan. Intertwined. It's… poetic, in a sense."

He stared at her, eyes wide, panic sharpening every line in his face. "Jane… what are you saying?"

Jane leaned back, tilting her head as she studied him. "I'm saying… the girl you destroyed is gone. She is not here. There is only this, this hollow, cold, relentless version of me. And she's… free. But not empty. Not weak. Not remorseful. Not… human, as you would understand it. She is what you created. And she likes it."

A shiver ran down Stefan's spine. For the first time, fear was mingled with recognition. He could see the pattern, the mirror of himself. She had become everything he had become, only sharper, faster, more patient.

Jane's voice softened, almost reflective. "I'm not sorry, Stefan. I feel… nothing. Nothing but clarity, relief… and… something darker. Excitement. Power. A release that I never thought I'd experience. But it isn't joy. Not happiness. Not the old Jane."

Her eyes swept over him, scanning every flinch, every tremor. The quiet room became a stage, each heartbeat a drumbeat of anticipation. The knife in her hand glimmered, not a weapon in the traditional sense, but a reflection of the precision, the cruelty, the obsession that had guided her for months.

"And now," she whispered, leaning forward, voice low and deliberate, "I know what it's like to wield control. To shape fear. To watch someone tremble, not out of survival, but understanding. The way you made me tremble, Stefan… I make you tremble now. I am the monster you created. And I am awake."

Stefan's chest heaved. His eyes darted to the knife, then to her, then back to the shadows that seemed to move on their own. His pulse roared in his ears. He had lived on fear, had controlled it, and now it engulfed him entirely.

Jane's fingers brushed the handle of the knife. Not striking. Not yet. But the movement was deliberate, a silent demonstration of the line she had crossed.

A laugh escaped her lips, quiet, brittle, and startling in the small room. Not malicious. Not triumphant. Not human. Only… delighted and empty.

"You see, Stefan," she murmured, gaze fixed on him, "the monster… always wins in the end. It just wears different faces. And tonight, it wears mine."

Her eyes drifted to the knife. She could feel it, the weight, the coldness, the reflection of her own face. In that reflection, she did not see herself, she only saw the shadow of Stefan, the shadow of everything she had sworn to destroy, and the shadow of what she had become.

A tremor ran through her, not from fear, but from recognition. She was the end of the story. She was the consequence. She was the predator. And yet… inside her, something fragile, something human, whispered that the cycle could not stop here.

She raised the knife, the metal cold, a mirror of the emptiness she felt. Her hand hovered, quivering slightly, not from hesitation, but from the gravity of understanding.

I must stop myself now, she thought but she couldn't.

The tip of the knife found Stefans's chest, almost trembling with anticipation.

Outside, the city was slowly waking. Horns, footsteps, distant laughter. Life continuing, unaware. Indifferent as she slowly added weight to the knife.

She felt a strange thrill, almost alien, the echo of Stefan in herself, precise, cold, and unrelenting. It was familiar, and terrifying, and it made her smile.

The blade pressed down as if it knew its own path, finding the hollow between ribs, the spaces that mattered most. Jane felt detached, almost floating above herself, watching the motion as if it belonged to someone else, precise, inevitable, clinical. A sharp warmth began to bloom beneath her fingers, a heady, intoxicating surge that made the edges of the room shimmer. Her pulse raced, exhilaration and horror tangled into something dangerous, almost euphoric. And then it came, the shock of heat, the undeniable reality of blood. It snapped her from the haze, and the world reasserted itself with a violent clarity.

She dropped the knife. It clattered against the floor. The sound echoed like a bell, final and hollow. She slumped back in her chair, the shadows stretching across her face.

Inside, the room was still. Two hearts had been, now only one. One pulse thudding in her ears. One shadow in the dim light. One fractured mind staring at itself.

And then a heartbeat. Not hers. No longer his. Somewhere beneath the walls, the city, the sky. Somewhere… undetermined.

Jane's eyes widened. She listened. The world held its breath.

Is this how it ends with the moment between heartbeats, suspended, unresolved, terrifyingly infinite.

Chapter 14
Edge of Echoes

The room was alive. Not metaphorically, but alive.

Shadows twisted in the corners, thick as smoke, curling and stretching, brushing against walls and floor as though searching for her pulse. The lamp above buzzed, flickered, stuttered, then steadied for a heartbeat, casting fractured light that spilled across the knife in her lap. Reflections scattered: her face, Stefan's grin, Emily's pale eyes. A hall of mirrors folding endlessly, reality devouring itself.

Outside, rain smothered the glass in restless sheets. For a moment, something darker moved through it, a shape turning toward the window. Or maybe it was only the storm shifting its weight. When the lamp flickered again, it was gone.

She had killed him. Stefan's final pulse had fluttered beneath her fingers, the warmth of life surrendering to the cold inevitability of steel. It had been deliberate, necessary, almost merciful. But when his breath stopped, something in her had started. His echo. His rhythm. His cruelty. It had seeped into her veins, quiet at first, then rising like a tide.

Now, she could feel him in everything, the hum of the lamp, the crawl of the shadows, the flicker of reflections on the walls.

The room shifted with each exhale, breathing alongside her. The floor rippled. The ceiling bowed low. The walls leaned inward, listening. Each flicker of light birthed new reflections that multiplied without mercy: Stefan's smile, Emily's eyes, her own trembling mouth. They merged, unmerged, blurred into something monstrous.

Her laughter cracked the air thin, brittle, wrong. It wasn't hers. It wasn't his. It belonged to something else that had grown between them, a third voice, sharp, deliberate, patient. The knife trembled in her palm, humming faintly, as if it too remembered.

"I am the monster," she whispered. Her voice fractured like glass. "The thing I swore I would end… and yet I remain. Stefan's shadow. His echo. And now… his heir."

A flicker in the corner. Too quick, too human. Stefan's grin flashed, puppet like, eyes stretched too wide, fingers twitching as if pulled by invisible strings. Then gone. A ghost. A thought. It didn't matter. He was inside her now. His patience coiled in her muscles; his cruelty nested in her mind.

Time loosened. Seconds stretched into threads and snapped. The lamp shuddered. Shadows quivered, whispering her name, or his. The reflections deepened, spiralling. Emily's terrified face appeared between them, beneath the tree she remembered too well, mouth open in silent pleading.

"Emily," Jane breathed, though her voice barely sounded like language.

The reflection's lips moved, but no sound came. Her eyes glistened, not angry. Pleading. Not for life, but for release.

Lightning tore through the window, searing every surface in white. For an instant, the world existed in impossible layers, Emily's eyes, Stefan's grin, Jane's fever bright stare, stacked on top of each other like mismatched transparencies.

Then, the sound.

A *tap*.

Soft. Rhythmic. From the window.

She froze. The knife stilled in her lap. Another *tap*, gentle, almost polite. A shadow moved beyond the glass, distorted by rain. Human? Imagination? The lamp flickered violently, throwing shards of light across her reflection. She couldn't tell if the tapping was real or the echo of her heartbeat.

The shadow tilted its head, watching. Waiting.

"Stefan?" she whispered. "Emily?"

No answer. Only another *tap*.

Her chest tightened. The sound threaded itself into the rhythm of the room, the buzz of the lamp, the pulse in her veins, the hum in her skull. It all merged, a single, suffocating cadence.

The knife was cold in her palm. Electric. Alive. It knew her as she knew it, intimately, ritualistically. She dragged it slowly along her thigh, not to cut, but to remember. To measure the distance between who she was and what she had become. Each heartbeat was an echo of another: hers, Stefan's, Emily's, indistinguishable now.

"I am the monster," she said again, steadier this time. "I am Stefan's creation. I am the thing I swore to destroy. And yet…"

She swallowed the words. They burned.

"…I still exist."

The shadows leaned closer, feeding on the tremor in her voice. The walls bent inward, the air vibrating with her pulse. The room had become a lung, breathing, tightening, consuming. The knife gleamed like a vein of silver in the flickering dark.

The tapping at the window came once more, soft, uncertain, almost like a heartbeat trying to match hers.

Her laughter returned, quieter now, breaking at the edges. It wasn't madness; it was release. Recognition. The sound rippled through the room, merged with the hum of the lamp, the hiss of the storm, the whisper of shadows.

The knife rose, steady in her trembling hand. Hovering at her throat. Cold. Electric. Inevitable. The air around it thickened, pulsing in sync with her heart. She pressed the blade lightly, not to end, not yet, but to acknowledge. To greet the final truth.

The walls breathed. The floor heaved. The lamp froze mid flicker, holding the moment in an impossible stillness.

Every reflection caught that light. Emily beneath the tree. Stefan's hollow grin. Jane's trembling face. And behind it all, one shadow outside the window, unmoving. Watching.

One final heartbeat pressed against her skull, too loud, too heavy. Hers? His? The rooms? Or something waiting beyond the glass? Impossible to know.

"Maybe I haven't escaped at all. Maybe the darkness just learned my name...."

And in that suffocating pause, Jane realized, the knife was waiting.

But her freedom... it would not.

Author's Note

Some stories don't begin with imagination…they begin with the things we carry.

The wounds we don't speak about. The shadows that follow quietly behind us.

The truths we survive but never walk away from unchanged.

Hunting Stefan was written with that in mind.

This book is fiction, but the emotions inside it…fear, obsession, the slow work of rebuilding a life after it's been broken, are very real for many people. Trauma does not end where the world thinks it should. Survival is not a finish line. It is a long, uneven path in the dark, and no two people walk it the same way.

Jane's journey is not meant to mirror anyone's reality, but to echo a truth:

that the mind is a fragile, powerful place, and healing is rarely a straight line.

If you recognized these patterns, either personally or through someone you know, please remember this:

recovery is not linear, and survival is not synonymous with healing.

Thank you for stepping into the dark with her.

And thank you for stepping back out.

www.ingramcontent.com/pod-product-compliance
Lightning Source LLC
LaVergne TN
LVHW050937080826
845145LV00004B/1295

* 9 7 8 1 8 0 6 4 5 0 2 5 1 *